For Oscar, Mateo and Mimi – L.S.

First published in 2022 by Scholastic Children's Books
Euston House, 24 Eversholt Street, London, NW1 1DB
Scholastic Ireland, 89E Lagan Road, Dublin Industrial Estate, Glasnevin, Dublin, D11 HP5F

HB ISBN: 978 07023 1433 9
PB ISBN : 978 07023 0348 7

A CIP catalogue record for this book is available from the British Library.

Printed in China
Paper made from wood grown in sustainable forests and other controlled sources.

3 5 7 9 10 8 6 4 2

www.scholastic.co.uk

SCHOLASTIC

Search, renew or reserve
www.buckinghamshire.gov.uk/libraries

24 hour renewal line
0303 123 0035

Library enquiries
01296 382415

...mshire Libraries and Culture

...veyourlibrary

@BucksLibraries

LORNA SCOBIE

I WOULD RATHER

HUG A TIGER

I am always being asked to do the most BORING things.

It is SO much more fun to be adventurous.

The trouble is, there are just SO MANY boring things.

We are going now, Small Panda! Please can you brush your fur?

Please can you wash your face and paws?

Please can you put away your train?

And there's ALWAYS something much more exciting to do ...

The grown-ups don't mind as they have so many BORING things to be getting on with.

NO THANK YOU! We would rather come to yours!

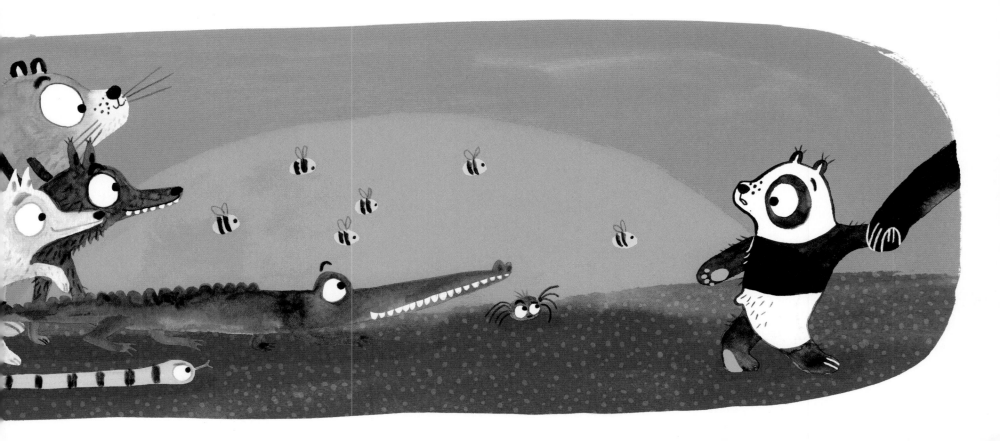

Maybe the BORING things aren't so bad after all.

And even an adventurer enjoys bedtime stories.

Night, night. Are you going to sleep now, too?

Thank you, but I'm not going to sleep. I would RATHER...

Because we ALL like doing adventurous things sometimes, don't we!